THE
BODYGUARD

pa

THE BODYGUARD

Sean Rodman

orca soundings

ORCA BOOK PUBLISHERS

Library and Archives Canada Cataloguing in Publication

Rodman, Sean, 1972–, author
The bodyguard / Sean Rodman.
(Orca soundings)

Issued in print and electronic formats.
ISBN 978-1-4598-2201-6 (softcover).—ISBN 978-1-4598-2202-3 (PDF).—
ISBN 978-1-4598-2203-0 (EPUB)

I. Title. II. Series: Orca soundings
PS8635.O355B63 2019   jC813'.6   C2018-904882-4
C2018-904883-2

First published in the United States, 2019
Library of Congress Control Number: 2018954080

Summary: In this high-interest novel for teen readers,
a star football player who dreams of being a filmmaker
agrees to be an exchange student's bodyguard.

*Orca Book Publishers is dedicated to preserving the environment and
has printed this book on Forest Stewardship Council® certified paper.*

Orca Book Publishers gratefully acknowledges the support for its
publishing programs provided by the following agencies: the Government of
Canada, the Canada Council for the Arts and the Province of British Columbia
through the BC Arts Council and the Book Publishing Tax Credit.

Edited by Tanya Trafford
Cover images by iStock.com/digitalskillet (front) and
Shutterstock.com/Krasovski Dmitri (back)

ORCA BOOK PUBLISHERS
orcabook.com

Printed and bound in Canada.

22 21 20 19 • 4 3 2 1

To Laura. I couldn't do it without you.

Chapter One

My name is Ryan "Replay" Hale. According to the local newspaper, I'm the greatest running back that Marathon High School has ever seen. The *Marathon Tribune* called me a "talent to watch." And "the golden boy of the Golden Warriors."

But they don't know about my pregame ritual—barfing quietly in a

Sean Rodman

locker-room bathroom stall, hoping nobody hears me. The only one who does hear me, unfortunately, is my best friend, Alex. He always stands guard outside.

"Replay?" he hisses through the stall door. "You almost finished? Game time in five."

My empty stomach lurches again, trying to hurl whatever might be left down there into the stained toilet bowl in front of me. The result of a nasty cocktail of nerves and fear. Not for the first time I wonder at the cruel joke of genetics that made me into a football superman. I'd much prefer to be Clark Kent. I have a love-hate thing with the game of football.

I'm distracted from my misery by muffled voices outside the stall door.

"Replay must have had a bad burrito, Coach," I overhear Alex say. "No big deal, sir. He'll be right out."

2

Alex thumps on the door. "Seriously, man! Ride the vomit comet and get out here."

There's no more putting it off. I can't disappoint Alex. My team. My parents. I wipe my mouth with the back of a gloved hand and adjust my neck roll. My stomach feels like it's filled with battery acid. But it's time for my game face. I slide my helmet on, hoping it will hide my seasick expression, and open the stall door.

"Replay! Good to see you, man!" Alex checks his watch and raises an eyebrow. "Seventeen minutes and thirty-seven seconds of solid puke." His teeth flash white as he grins and slaps me on my shoulder pads. We walk out of the locker room and through the dim tunnel toward the brightly lit field. He's chuckling to himself all the way.

"What are you so happy about?" I ask. As we step out of the tunnel, the noise and sights of the field make Alex pause before answering. The big screen is flashing a pre-game show, throwing crazy shadows everywhere. The stands are like rippling sheets of gold, Warriors fans decked out in our school colors. It feels like a circus with the drums banging away and cheerleaders spinning and twirling, all blond hair and wide smiles.

We walk over to our place on the bench. It's occupied by a new guy, a freshman. Alex gives him the hard stare until he shoves over. Star treatment for the star players, like me and him. I guess football has some perks.

"Why am I happy, you ask? Well, I'm proud of you, son." Alex puts a fatherly hand on my shoulder.

"Proud of me? For what?"

"That was your personal best for a pregame spew-fest. The more you barf, the better you play. I've watched you do this for what, a dozen games?" He gives me a toothy grin. "Bet you didn't know this, but I timed all your barf-o-thons."

"That's actually kinda creepy."

"No, no. I'm a scientist, man. I have the data to back me up now. It's not just a theory. Longer barf session equals better game performance. It's a fact. You're going to be awesome on the field tonight." Alex suddenly looks serious and leans in toward me. The crowd roars louder. "Just don't lose your lunch while you're wearing your helmet. That'll get ugly."

"Thanks for the advice, man." Time for the other part of my pre-game ritual. I pull out a small video camera from my backpack under the bench. "Also, how come you know so many words for 'puke'? How many can there be?"

"Challenge accepted, my friend! Let's see…there's *blow chunks. Toss a sidewalk pizza. Chunder. Curl and hurl. Drive the porcelain bus…*"

I tune Alex out and flip open the little screen on the side of the camera. Pressing the red Record button, I scan the field. Two lines of players. We're in gold, they're in white. The quarterback barks out his call, then snaps the ball forward. Game on. I pan over to the stands. The drummers in front, thrashing away on their instruments. Behind and above them, rows and rows of fans wearing gold-colored T-shirts and hats. I pause for a moment and zoom in on a middle-aged couple, cheering frantically. They're dressed in matching oversized Golden Warriors T-shirts and shimmery gold wigs. I groan softly. Mom and Dad. Hard-core football fans. Unlike myself. I click off the camera and put it back into my pack. I realize the new guy is studying me, wide blue eyes under a mop of blond hair. What is he, like, ten years old?

"You getting game tape or something?" he asks. "So you can study it later? That is so pro."

I shrug. The truth is that just seeing everything through the camera screen kind of calms me down, gives me some distance. I like movies, real life or made up.

Alex stops listing all the words for puke to answer the new guy. "Yeah, he tapes every damn thing, all the damn time. That's why we call him Replay." Alex shakes his head "You have so much to learn, newbie. Go get us some Gatorade."

Coach comes over. He never walks, runs or hustles, no matter what's happening on the field. He saunters like some old-timey cowboy. He bends down to look me in the eye. "Ryan, you gonna make us proud today?"

"Yes, sir."

"Then get out there. It's your time to shine." He slaps me on the helmet.

I trot onto the field along the solid wall of linesmen. The play is called a draw. Designed for a high-speed running back such as myself, it relies on a couple of things to work. First, my big refrigerator-shaped friends— like Alex—need to block the opposing refrigerator-shaped linesmen and pin them down. Then I have to spot a hole in the grunting mass of players and shoot through it, like a turbo-powered slippery eel. If everything goes right, we gain some yardage. If not, I get crushed under hundreds of pounds of irate refrigerators. I belch into my helmet, wincing at the stench.

As I squat into position directly behind the quarterback, I hear him make the call. In a moment, the QB has the ball and is pedaling backward toward me. He's making it look like he might throw a long pass down the field. Instead I rush up toward him, and as I sprint by, the QB stuffs the ball into my waiting arms. I quickly scan the field and panic a little. No holes to shoot through. I swerve and keep running, hoping something will open up. Nothing. I can practically touch the wall of linesmen struggling ahead of me. Nothing.

And then it happens. Players peel off to the left and right, tumbling to the ground. There's my window through the line. One guy leaps out of nowhere, but he's timed his tackle too early. He skids into the grass right at my feet. I lift off, leaping over him like he's a big, stanky speed bump. And then I'm on the other side of the line, free and hurtling down the field. The crowd roars around me. Players on both teams, white and gold, are tearing after me. But I cannot be stopped. I am pure momentum. I am a rocket, a meteor, tearing across the green sky of the field.

For a moment there, I think football is pretty all right. Then my legs get pulled out from under me, and I pinwheel into the ground. My face slams against the front of my helmet, and I taste metal in my mouth. A second later a refrigerator lands on my back. But the crowd is going wild, because I've gained some serious yardage for my team. They're chanting my name: "Replay! Replay!"

Like I said, I have a love-hate thing going with the game of football.

Chapter Two

"Why does the computer lab always smell like moldy cheese?"

Following Alex's lead, I take a cautious sniff. I've never noticed it before, but he's right. Dirty socks or wet dog. Weird. But it sort of fits in with the general vibe of the broken-down computer lab. A bunch of old whirring boxes attached to smudged screens that kinda-sorta work. The walls are decorated with posters suggesting we learn to code or study engineering, peeling slowly away from the wall. It's a sunny day outside, and it seems criminal to be stuck in this cheesy-smelling, despair-filled room.

The guidance counselor, Mr. Pier, is working his way around the class, logging everybody into a website designed to "give us feedback on possible career choices." Eventually Alex and I start filling out screen after screen of questions:

I would rather be (choose one):
(a) audit manager
(b) a safety manager

"I would rather (c) punch myself in the head," whispers Alex. I snicker.

I enjoy hobbies I can do on my own, such as gardening or developing photographs.   (True/False)

"Developing photographs?" hisses Alex. "I think my gramps did that when he was a kid. Right after he used his telegraph."

I would rather be (choose one):
(a) an artist
(b) an athlete

The smile fades from my face. It's not a real choice, is it? If you want to make art—say, movies—guess what happens? You starve to death. "Artist" is not a real job. Being an athlete, on the other hand, can get you places. College on a full-ride scholarship, for example. A career with the NFL. Using your talents as an investment in your future.

"You all right?" Alex is looking at me, his big forehead crinkled in concern. "I mean, you're looking at that screen like it gave you 'psycho killer' as your future career."

I punch him in the shoulder, a little harder than I mean to. Alex swears in surprise, which draws the attention of Mr. Pier.

"Mr. Martinez?" he says to Alex. "Do we have a problem?"

"No, sir. Sorry. I've finished the quiz. What do I do now?"

"Just be patient. The software is combining your academic transcripts with your answers. I'll print out a copy of your report when it's done. That way you can share it with your parents."

As Mr. Pier walks toward the printer, Alex turns to me. "What has got you wound so tight, man?"

"I don't know. Graduation, college, jobs. It's all really…complicated."

"Complicated?" Alex looks confused. "We are legendary football players! Colleges want legendary football players. Colleges have money. We don't have money. We will take their money. And we will be kings!" He lifts both hands in the air, victorious, like he just spiked the ball in the end zone.

"King Alex?" Mr. Pier says dryly, reappearing over his shoulder. "Your enthusiasm for career planning is impressive. But dial down the volume. Here are your reports."

"Hey! *Stand-up comedian*!" says Alex, reading the first page. "That's awesome! I can do that. And radio announcer? Like a DJ? All right!"

"I'm thinking you may not have taken the quiz seriously, Alex," says Mr. Pier. Just then the bell rings. There's a roar of chairs scraping and feet stampeding for the door. I nod at Mr. Pier, and we make our escape.

Alex and I shoulder through the crowd toward our lockers.

"DJ Alex Martinez!" he yells over the top of all the heads. "I like the sound of that!" He mimes spinning records, scratching back and forth.

We reach our lockers, clearing a couple of juniors out of the way with hard stares. I undo the padlock and slam the thin metal door open.

"Seriously, dude?" I say. "You're definitely not a comedian. And I can't see you being a DJ. Like you said, we're going to play ball."

"Hey!" Alex suddenly spins me around and pushes me against the lockers. He looks fierce. He shoves one finger into my chest.

"Remember, music chose me—not the other way around. Music is not what I do. It's who I am. Twenty-four hours a day, eight days a week, broadcasting the live beats all around the world!"

His face splits into a wide grin. "Damn, Replay! Lighten up! You are taking this crap way too seriously! You know it doesn't mean anything, right?"

"Okay, maybe I was wrong," I say. "The comedian thing sort of works for you."

Alex pretends to straighten up my T-shirt and dust it off. "You know it. Now let's get to practice. That'll get you thinking straight again."

Chapter Three

The first time I see Markus I'm headed down the hallway, my sneakers squeaking on the concrete floor. He's wearing beige pants with neat creases— my gramps would call them slacks—a white dress shirt and a gray jacket that almost reaches his knees. His clothes look expensive but awkward somehow, like someone else chose his entire outfit.

I overhear him talking to Emily and Mina, two girls from the cheerleading squad. He has a thick accent that has a sort of singsong quality to it.

"I was kind of a big deal," he says. "I mean, it wasn't like I was super famous for playing poker. But I was, you know, almost super famous?" The girls are smiling, but they have this look on their faces like he's been talking at them for a while now. The curiosity is wearing off. Emily sees me out of the corner of her eye and seizes the opportunity.

"Hey, Replay! Come meet the new kid," she says brightly. "Sorry, what was your name again?"

"Markus," he says. He thrusts out a hand for me to shake like he's stabbing me with a knife. I carefully take it, and he pumps up and down a few times. His palm feels wet and cold. Markus blinks behind his thick glasses and studies me.

"You play football here?" he asks. "You look very strong."

Emily looks at me and rolls her eyes. "Sweetie, he is one of the best football players in town." She smiles. "In fact, he can tell you all about football. Mina and I have to get to practice. See ya!" Emily and Mina swing their backpacks over their shoulders and hustle off down the hallway.

Markus smiles tightly. "Uh, I did not play football in my home country. I was not an athlete so much."

Looking at his scrawny frame, I can understand that. "You're the new exchange student?" I ask.

He nods. "Before coming here, I was studying in Estonia. You know Estonia?"

"Estonia? That's, like, *Lord of the Rings*, right?"

"No." He blinks and slowly shakes his head. "It is a very small country close to Russia. On the Baltic Sea? Next to Latvia?" Markus can see that I have no idea what he is talking about. "It's okay. It's okay. Most people don't know where it is. You have lived in Marathon a long time?"

"All my life. Born and bred."

"You like it? It's a pretty small town, no?" Markus says.

"Well, it's all right. Probably still bigger than Estonia."

Markus laughs, which startles me. It's a kind of a half snort, half wheeze with a hint of honk thrown in at the end. I see Markus look past my shoulder and nod. "That teacher wants you, I think."

I turn around and see Mr. Pier hovering, a paper in his hand.

"Thank you, Markus," Mr. Pier says. "Can I have a word with Replay, uh, Ryan?" The nickname is stuck onto me so bad even the teachers can't help but use it.

"Yes, sir," says Markus. He closes up his locker. "Excuse me, Reply. I will see you around and later."

Mr. Pier waits for him to leave. "Nice to see you're helping Markus out. He seems a little awkward," he says.

"I'm not really helping him so much as—" I say.

Mr. Pier cuts me off. "Replay, listen, I was surprised by your results from the quiz today. And then I looked at your answers. I know lots of students cheat on tests. But I've never come across someone cheating on a career quiz."

"Mr. Pier, I'm not sure what you mean. I didn't copy anyone else." I feel myself hardening up, like I'm bracing for a hit. "How do you even cheat on a career quiz?"

"That's kind of what I mean. I think the answers you gave are not, well, the answers you really *wanted* to give.

I've watched you at this school for years. You've shown tremendous talent for two things, football and making movies. I think your talent is outstanding, and I think you should follow that dream if that's what you want."

"I know everyone says I've got a gift," I say. "So that's what I wrote on the quiz. That I'm going for a football scholarship. That I'm an athlete."

"No." Mr. Pier shakes his head. "That's not the talent I meant. I was talking about filmmaking. I've seen what you've done for class projects and for the student art festival. You're really good."

He hands me the sheet of paper. I assume it's more career-planning stuff. It's not. The top of the first page reads *UCLA School of the Motion Picture Arts*. It's an application. There are several pages full of lots of questions and boxes.

I fold the paper up and stuff it into the back pocket of my jeans. Mr. Pier is looking at me.

"That's nice of you to say, Mr. Pier." I shrug. "But making movies isn't a real job, is it? And I've got a recruiter coming to interview me this weekend. It's like my dad says—I'm destined to play ball."

"That doesn't have to be the only thing you do," Mr. Pier says, smiling. "And there are scholarships you can apply for as well. It was a bit harsh of me to say you cheated on that quiz. But you should always tell the truth on a test like that. Otherwise, you're just lying to yourself."

I mumble an awkward thank-you, sling my backpack and turn away from him. I merge into the moving stream of students, losing myself in the flow toward the football field.

Chapter Four

I arrive home with sweat-sticky skin and a growling stomach. Dad is just putting four plates on the table. In the middle is a big tray of roast chicken and potatoes. Dad's a big guy. It's easy to see how he would have been a terror on the football field in high school. All these years later, all his linebacker menace has morphed into something more like a big teddy bear. His face splits into a toothy smile when he sees me.

"Ryan! How was practice?"

"Brutal." I nab a potato off the tray and pop it into my mouth. Mom comes out of the kitchen and frowns at me.

"But you worked hard?" Dad asks.

I roll my eyes, but I actually like that I get the exact same question after every practice.

"The hardest, Dad. The hardest. Do I have time for a shower?"

"After. Sit down and eat while it's hot," says Mom. She's as small and thin as Dad is broad and tall. She carefully sets a napkin over her lap—she hasn't changed out of her work clothes from her day at the bank. I sit down with my parents, noticing the empty fourth chair at the table.

"Where's Amber?"

"Who knows? Not like she ever calls with that fancy phone we bought her." Dad starts to load up his plate with food, then pauses. "You remember that Mr. Howards is coming on Saturday for lunch, right?"

"How could I forget? You guys bring it up every night." Ever since the recruiter from Ryeburn College called and asked to meet with us, my parents have been like little kids waiting for Christmas. Counting down the days.

"Well, it's a big opportunity. I don't want you to waste it."

"I know." I push some green broccoli toward a pool of gravy on my plate. "So I was thinking about what I should talk to Mr. Howards about when he's here. I mean, besides football. Like my other interests."

Mom blinks and tilts her head a little. "Like what?"

"I don't know. Like my movies. It might give him a better idea of who I am. What else I bring to the college."

"What you bring to the college is your god-given talent, Ryan," Mom says. "Never doubt that."

"Besides, it's not like you're going to study moviemaking at college. It's a hobby, not a job. Like your uncle Simon and his music. He keeps thinking he'll be some big-shot drummer in a band. Meanwhile, he's spending his life on the till at Costco. Might just die there."

Mom looks uncomfortable. "That's not fair, is it? My brother had some tough breaks."

Dad's response is interrupted by the door banging open. Amber tumbles through it, an avalanche of brown frizzy hair, binders and shopping bags.

Dad puts down his fork and knife, eyes narrowing. "You're late."

"I was studying with Shannon." She drops her jacket in the hallway and comes to the table. "She has the coolest app on her phone for messaging. I want to get it."

"Messaging? Like, texting? I don't see why you need another way to talk to your friends on your phone," says Dad. He points a fork at her. "It's already a phone. That lets you talk. To your friends."

"You don't understand! Nobody actually talks on their phone anymore. And messaging on Facebook or Instagram is old news. The new thing is Yopeep."

"And this is why I bought you a phone? So you could Instabook your friends?" Dad knows perfectly well what Instagram is. He just likes to get a reaction. But he's on a roll now. "I bought you a phone so you could call your parents and let us know where you are. And when you are coming home to eat dinner with your family. And you never bother."

"Dad, you're so..." Amber slams her fork down on the table. "I'm just asking for an app. All my friends have it. And Ryan too, which is so unfair!"

"Way to throw me under the bus," I mumble around a mouthful of potatoes. "I hardly use Instabook at all."

Mom tries to calm everyone down. "Amber *is* thirteen. Maybe we should talk about this." She shrugs her shoulders and locks eyes with dad. That's Mom code for "you're being kind of a jerk."

"Okay, then. You're right. She's growing up. I guess Amber can have a YoBookFace account." Dad makes it sound like a royal proclamation. "On one condition."

"Really?" Ambers looks a little stunned. She's been working on getting this app for a month. A less honest kid—like, say, me—would have run out of patience and simply installed the app on the down-low. Here she is, winning over Dad. "What's the deal?"

"The condition is that I will set up the account for you," says Dad. "To make sure it's safe."

"That seems fair," says Mom quickly.

"Wait," says Amber. "You won't even let me set up my own—"

"Take it or leave it," says Dad. "It's a one-time offer. We'll do it right now or not at all."

"Fine." Amber pulls her phone out of the pocket of her hoodie, unlocks it and slides it across the dining table to Dad. Mom scooches her chair over so the two of them can stare at the screen. Dad squints at the tiny screen, then puts on his reading glasses. He stabs at the screen with a finger.

"Okay. New account. Uh-huh. Choose a unique user name. Nine characters maximum." He looks over his reading glasses at Amber.

"QTChick66," she says confidently. "I use it for all my accounts."

"No way," says Dad. "That's a terrible name."

"Dad! So unfair!"

"Let's think a little more about this one." Mom's now flashing her special stare at Amber, who just growls. Mom ignores it and says, "How about Buttons?"

"Wait—Buttons?" That makes me put down my fork and knife. "I forgot that you used to call her that."

"Because she was cute as a button." Dad crinkles his nose, his tough-guy image vanishing for a moment.

"That is *so* not okay," says Amber. "I will be teased to death by everyone at school. Literally."

"Literally?" I say. "I don't think that's technically possible, Buttons."

"Now hang on," says Dad. "She's right. We can improve on Buttons."

"Cool Buttons?" says Mom. "Awesome Buttons?"

"I've got it," says Dad. He quickly taps the screen.

"No!" says Amber as she lunges across the table.

Dad gives her a fierce look, and she promptly plops back down in her chair.

"Mind your manners, young lady," he says. "I present to you FunkyButtons. Your new Yopeep account name. Safely set up and ready to go." He holds the phone out to Amber. "Look, it's already sent a message to all your contacts."

Amber snatches it and swipes the screen. She stares at it for a long moment.

"Oh no!" she cries.

Mom and Dad look at each other.

"You don't get it. It's a maximum of *nine* letters for your user name," Amber says. "So it cuts off everything after the ninth letter."

"Yeah, so?" Dad starts counting off on his fingers. "F-u-n-k-y-B-u-t-t—oh."

"FunkyButt?" I say. I start laughing. "You just messaged everybody as FunkyButt?"

Nobody else is laughing.

"I'm literally going to die of embarrassment." Amber drops the phone on the table like it's contaminated. She drops her head into her hands. "Literally."

"Technically, I still don't think that's poss—" I break off when I see the crazy look on Amber's face. The one that tells you a whirlwind is coming.

There's a moment of silence, a single heartbeat. Then Amber starts screaming, Dad starts yelling, and I get out of there as fast as I can. I make a quick pit stop at the dishwasher to drop off my plate and then I'm up the stairs two at a time, still laughing. FunkyButt. Awesome.

Safely inside my room, I flop onto my bed, slide my headphones on and dial up my music to drown out the mayhem downstairs. Something feels weird in the pocket of my jeans. I reach around and grab the crumpled paper. The application form. Reading it over, my heart starts to thump in my chest. Film school. I could learn how to make real movies instead of just screwing around. But as I really read over the form, that feeling vanishes. I have to submit a sample of my work. I've got lots of little clips, one or two projects for school—but all of it is junk, really. I mean, *I* like it. People like Mr. Pier sometimes say nice things. But honestly, I haven't made anything that would be good enough for applying to film school.

Plus, at the bottom of the form it says that there's an application fee. It's $150 just to apply! I don't have that much in the bank. I had a job at the car wash, but I spent pretty much everything that came in. No way could I ask my parents to pay. They've made it pretty clear how they feel about me pursuing anything other than a football down the field.

I fold the paper back up again and drop it over the side of the bed. I close my eyes and drift off to sleep. Film school is a nice dream. Just a dream though.

Chapter Five

I'm running late, sprinting around the west parking lot of Marathon High to get to class. I'm hauling around a corner when I hear a voice say, "You're full of crap."

That makes me hit the brakes.

It's a kid in a black trench coat, his thin face twisted with a sneer. He's not speaking to me. He has the weird new kid, Markus, backed up against the wall. The two of them are tucked away in a kind of alcove, out of the sight of anyone else. Trench Coat clearly thought he had a spot where he could terrorize Markus unseen. Then I showed up.

The two of them swivel their heads to look at me. Markus grins. Trench Coat looks a little less pleased.

"Reply!" says Markus. "I am most happy to see you again!"

For a moment I consider my options. Keep running to class and leave Markus to get eaten up by the Not-So-Big Bad Wolf. Or step in, play cop, break up this little scene before it becomes serious and risk getting another late slip. Honestly, neither option is appealing. I settle for something in between.

"Dude, don't be a jerk," I say firmly to Trench Coat. Then I leave them to sort it out.

Before I make it more than a dozen steps, I hear Markus squeal. It sounds like a cat with a stepped-on tail. Damn.

I pull a quick turn and run back to the alcove. Sure enough, Trench Coat now has Markus down on the ground. He pulls a fancy-looking phone out of a pocket in Markus's expensive gray jacket.

"Seriously?" I drop my binder. "What did I just say?"

Trench Coat's face goes pale as he stands up and backs himself against the concrete wall. He doesn't let go of Markus's phone though.

"I gave you some good advice, didn't I?" I growl.

Trench Coat nods. He swallows and licks his lips. The alcove is narrow enough that I can block it pretty nicely. He knows he's trapped.

"I gave you, like, inspirational advice. Didn't I?"

Trench Coat nods again, more slowly this time.

"And what *was* that advice?" I'm right up in his face now and can smell garlicky morning breath.

"Don't be a…?" He trails off.

"Jerk. That's right. That's Einstein-level wisdom, isn't it? So what are you going to do now?"

Trench Coat's eyes dart from my face to the phone in his hand. I gently pluck it from his sweaty grip.

"Not be a…?" Trench Coat whispers.

"Jerk. Smart. You know who I am?"

"Reply!" yells a voice behind us. "You are Reply, the football hero!"

For a second Trench Coat almost smirks. I stare him down and call out over my shoulder, "Markus, it's *Replay*. Not reply. Please stop talking."

I grind a finger into Trench Coat's forehead. "My name is Replay. As in,

I keep coming back again and again until I get what I want. As in, I'm going to loop back on you if you disrespect me. Understand?" Trench Coat has returned to looking nicely pale and terrified. I'm satisfied that my job is done. I step aside, and he scurries away.

Markus is still sitting on the pavement. He's looking at me with wide eyes. "You can be most scary."

He holds up one hand, looking pathetic. I grab it and pull him off the ground.

"Thanks, I guess," I say. I give him back his phone. As I do, I notice the time. I might still make it to class without a late slip.

As I start to leave, Markus yells, "Wait!"

"No, man, I have to get to class. If I'm late again, the coach can pull me from the next game." I scoop my binder off the ground and start to hustle out of the alcove, toward the side entrance of the school.

"I want to pay you!"

"What?" I stop and turn back to Markus. "I don't know what they do in Narnia or wherever you come from, but we don't pay people for stuff like that here. We just say thank you. It's okay."

"No, you misunderstand." Markus is smiling a sort of mad-scientist grin. "When I see how scary you can be, I realize I must offer you a business deal."

"I've really got to go. The teacher is—"

"I want you to be my bodyguard. I need protection."

I take a deep breath. I don't have time for this. "You'll be fine."

I leave but can hear him calling me. He's panting from trying to keep up.

"I will pay you. One hundred dollars. To be my bodyguard."

"No," I call out, not breaking stride.

"One hundred dollars. Each week."

My hands are on the metal handles, but I don't pull the doors open. One hundred dollars a week? That sounds like easy money. I think of the crumpled film-school application on the floor of my room. The application fee.

I let go of the door and slowly turn to face Markus. His nice clothes are rumpled and streaked with dirt. His brown hair looks like it's been styled with a rake, complete with a couple of leaves.

"One twenty-five," I say. "You really have the money?"

His smile is so bright it's like a searchlight flashing on. He stuffs a hand into a jacket pocket and pulls out a wallet. He starts counting out twenties.

"Sixty dollars up front. I pay you the rest at the end of the week."

He holds out the wad of bills.

"I stick to you like glue and paper, okay? You keep me safe?"

His eyes are wide. I have a sudden stab of guilt—I'm about to rip off a rich exchange student who just had a bad first day at school.

"Markus, you don't need to be afraid of anyone who goes to this school. Even that idiot in the trench coat. Most of them aren't like that at all. You don't need a bodyguard."

Markus's face grows serious, and he shakes his head. "I don't need a bodyguard to protect me from the students of this school. I know that they are just—as you say—jerks. There are other reasons. I can explain later." He wiggles the cash at me. "Please?"

I don't have time to figure this out. The money is good even if the kid is weird. Whatever. Let's do this.

I take the money. "Deal."

Chapter Six

Sneaking into class is easy. The art teacher, Ms. Darpola, is taking everyone outside to do some sketching, so there's chaos to cover me as I slip in. A small riot as everyone grabs from a big pile of clipboards, pencils and paper. The occasional eraser flying through the air. The kind of behavior you'd expect from a bunch of unimpressed teenagers who have just been told to go draw a tree. When Alex and I signed up for art, it wasn't because of our love of painting or anything. It was well known as a bird course, an easy grade. But it's turned out I enjoy it more than I thought I would. Most of the time.

A few minutes later, clipboards in hand, Alex and I are sitting on the grass. We stare at a big oak tree at the edge of the back field.

"How about you draw and I take a nap?" says Alex. "Because I got nothing. I am not vibing this tree." He tosses his clipboard to the side and flops on his back.

I pull my video camera out. I frame up Alex and hit *Record*. "Hey, you know that new Markus kid?"

Alex grunts from under the baseball cap he has pulled down over his face.

"He wants to pay me to be his bodyguard."

There's a muffled snort from Alex. I move the camera away from him, switching focus to a couple of kids running track in the distance.

"Like, real money," I say. "A hundred and twenty-five dollars a week."

"To be his bodyguard? What do you have to do for it?" Alex sits up and looks at me seriously. "Do you have to take a bullet for him?"

"Shut up. I know it sounds weird. Markus had a bad first day, got a little roughed up. I helped him out. Now he just wants me to hang around and look tough, I think."

Actually, I'm not entirely sure what Markus is expecting. Does he think I'm going to stand guard at his house all night? He's not that crazy. Is he? I shake my head.

"I'm just going to be like a security guard, I think," I say.

"Or a security blanket. Sounds like this new kid just bought himself a friend."

"Again, shut up."

In science class Alex fiddles with his Bunsen burner, turning it from a flapping yellow flame to a tight blue triangle. He turns to me, peering through his clear plastic protective goggles. With his massive frame squeezed into a little white lab coat, Alex looks like he mugged a scientist.

"This bodyguard gig. You need to be with him all the time?"

I nod. "At school, for sure. After school, I guess. I figure I'll do it for a couple weeks, make some money, then cut him loose."

"I guess it's all right for a baby-sitting gig," Alex says. "Wait, what about my party tonight? Does this mean you can't come?"

Just then Mr. Rupert walks by our table. We focus on the blue liquid in a test tube that's starting to turn a shade of pink. Apparently, that's what is supposed to happen, because Mr. Rupert congratulates us and moves on to the next group.

"Aw, crap." I sigh. Alex is throwing a banger tonight, while his family is away. It is going to be epic. His house has a big pool and has been the site of several legendary parties. Somehow his parents have never heard about them. "I'll talk to Markus."

"You cannot miss the party. Everyone is going to be there." Alex leans in so close his goggles are touching mine. Alex puts on a wheezy accent, like a mean old grandpa. "You are like a brother to me. This is about family."

"Stop being weird."

"You missed the reference. I've been watching those old *Godfather* movies. Like you told me to! You're right—they're really good." Alex turns on the accent again. "You better come tonight. It is an offer you cannot refuse."

Chapter Seven

Markus is sitting by himself in the cafeteria. His fancy clothes still look rumpled from this morning's hold-up. He's studying the screen of his laptop with a serious look. That changes when he looks up and sees me.

"Ripley!" he says, a smile breaking across his face. "I am so glad to see you."

"Uh-huh." I put my tray down across from him and sit. "Let me clear something up. It's Replay, all right? Not Reply or Ripley or whatever. *Replay*."

Markus's eyebrows squish together. "Replay? That does not make sense."

"It's a nickname, because I like to film stuff with my camera. I make movies for my friends about football or school or whatever. People say I'm in charge of the replay, so everyone can see what happened." I pull out my camera and show him some game footage on the tiny screen.

"Ah. You are like…" Markus pauses to think. "Like Steven Spielberg. Or J.J. Abrams." He looks at me carefully. "If they played football?"

"No, I'm nothing like those guys. I just mess around. Anyways, this deal we have. I want to get clear on a couple things. First, I'm going to be off duty sometimes. You know that, right?"

Markus closes the lid of his laptop. He picks up a paper cup of coffee and takes a sip.

"I pay you to be my bodyguard all the time."

"Yeah, but it's not like I'm going to sleep over at your house."

"Sleep over?" Markus looks surprised. "No. I am not a child. You meet me in the morning, we walk to school. When I am not in class, you are here. After school we are together."

"Yeah, but I've got football practice or training most nights."

"Then I will come to the field. Maybe I could train with you?"

I put my elbows on the table and rub my eyes. "We need to set some ground rules. Tonight, for example, I have to be somewhere."

"I will come with you. Where?"

"It's a party at my friend Alex's house. You wouldn't like it."

Markus crosses his arms. "A party? I think you do not take your job seriously."

"Yeah, that's another thing. I was being honest with you before. I really think you don't need my protection all the time. That trench-coat kid won't bug you again. You'll be—"

"Stop," says Markus. He motions for me to come closer. Then closer. We end up leaning together over our plates of food, which smell of broccoli and soap. He whispers, "I do need your protection. There is someone who wants to kill me."

We stare intently at each other. "Who?" I ask.

"The Plunger," whispers Markus.

I sigh. "You're saying a homicidal plumber wants to take you out?"

"I can't explain more," hisses Markus, "but I must be with you all the time. Even tonight." His eyes are intent on mine, his face pinched.

"All right, you and your craziness can come to the party. Just wear something more…" I wave at his fancy jacket and shirt. "Just chill. You need more chill."

Chapter Eight

We walk alongside the cars that line the quiet street. Shadowy tree arms reach over us. Even from a block away I can hear the *thump-thump* of music from Alex's house. I look at Markus and inspect him again.

"Are you sure you don't want to change? I can drive you back to your house."

"It is cool. Yes." Markus seems distracted, scanning the street around us with birdlike movements. He's wearing an expensive white shirt, black dress pants and shiny leather shoes. The overall effect is more "May I take your order?" than "Let's party!" Whatever. I've got bigger things to worry about.

"All right, let's go over the play again. You can stay with me, just keep it low-key. We get in, stick around for an hour, get out, nobody gets hurt. If anything goes sideways I'm going to call an audible, and you better follow."

Markus shoots me a puzzled look.

"It means that I'm the one calling the shots, and I can change the plan on the fly. If things are going really well, we might stay longer. If not, we'll bail. Either way, you do as I say. Okay?"

"Okay to the calling of an audible, I think," says Markus slowly. "You know,

57

Sean Rodman

the English here is not what I learned in school."

We arrive. You can tell Alex's dad owns a big construction firm. The house has massive sandstone walls, a terra-cotta roof, a fancy wrought-iron gate around the whole thing. We can hear the music more clearly now, as well as the sounds of splashing from the pool around back.

"I must warn you," says Markus as we close the gate behind us and start walking up toward the big wooden door. "When I am nervous, I start to talk very much. I feel like I must make people impressed with me."

"I noticed that the other day," I say. "Don't do that."

Before I can say anything else, the door swings open. It's Emily. "Replay, you made it!" She throws her arms around me, then steps back and looks at Markus. "And here you are too."

58

He bows to her, and Emily widens her eyes at me. "Well, that's more like it. Come on in."

The living room is packed. People are spilling out through open patio doors onto the pool deck. Alex has set himself up behind a pair of turntables. A stack of speakers flanks him on either side. He flashes a grin at me, then gets back to work on the beats. This party definitely has all the ingredients to be legendary.

Markus stays close to me as I drift around from group to group. I get into a detailed conversation with a linebacker, Curtis, about sack rates versus finishing drives. And the odds on the Patriots making it to the Super Bowl this year. When I look around, I spot Markus talking to a kid from my biology class. It's clearly a one-sided conversation. Markus is probably bragging about his poker days again. Fine. If he has found a semi-willing victim for his stories, I'm okay with that. I'm glad to be free of him for a little while. I can feel my shoulders unclench a little. This is working out.

The first sign of trouble comes about an hour into the party. I've pulled out my camera, and I'm getting some great footage. With a killer soundtrack underneath it, I can edit this into an awesome sequence. Then I overhear loud voices from the other side of the pool. It's Markus and Alex.

"I'm impressed," Alex is saying. "You don't seem the gangster type. And I've seen all the *Godfather* movies, so I'm all up on that."

"No, I am most gangster! Like I tell you, I spend time with real gangsters every day back home. But not Italian mob. Russian. I play poker with them. High stakes." Markus is speaking louder and louder, and I can see sweat stains creeping through his white waiter shirt. "I am one bad dude."

There's a crowd starting to form around them. "You do seem pretty bad," says one girl. "What were these poker games like? You have to fight for your life with a bunch of killers?" She makes her fingers into pistols and points them at Markus, smiling.

Markus completely misses the sarcasm in her voice. "It was online poker, so I did not meet the gangsters mostly. I met only one for real. But…" Markus hesitates. "I am certain he was a killer."

I can see this is a bad situation that is only going to get worse. I walk close to Markus and hiss, "You're talking too much. I'm calling an audible. Let's get out of here."

"No," says Markus firmly. "I am your boss, and I am fine." He even puts a hand on my chest and gently pushes me away.

Whatever. Keep talking, buddy.

"Did your killer have a good mob name?" asks Alex. "Like Scarface?"

"This was Russian mob," Markus continues. "He was the son of a *vor*, a boss. They called him…the Plunger."

Here we go.

"That is a terrible name for a gangster," Alex says. "Like, the thing you use to unplug a toilet?"

"No. The Plunger got his name because he liked to drown his victims by plunging them into the Hudson River," Markus says dramatically.

"Hold up," says Emily. "Where did you say you came from? Isn't the Hudson in…?" Nobody hears her though. They're all paying attention to Markus. But he is getting more and more agitated. His white shirt now has big rings of sweat under the armpits. His hair stands on end as he nervously rakes a hand through it. The owl-like glasses are fogging up.

Markus raises his voice. "I double-crossed the Plunger in a poker game. Cheated him of all his money. It was like taking a piece of cake from a baby." His braces twinkle in the patio lights, and spittle flies from his lips.

"Yeah, you seem like a real tough guy," says Curtis, the big linebacker I was talking to earlier. He turns to me. "Where did this jerk come from? Who let him in?"

I look at Markus, then to Curtis. "I have no idea. Never saw him before tonight." I didn't think Markus could hear me. But the look Markus shoots my way makes it clear that he did.

"Yo, Alex!" yells Curtis. "Turn up the tunes. I've had enough of this guy's crap." The crowd starts to drift away as the bass thumps louder. Eventually

Markus is left all alone. He slumps down onto a deck chair.

"They don't believe me," says Markus. "They don't like me." He lifts his head and looks at me with sad eyes. "You don't like me."

"Listen, Markus." I rub the back of my neck. "You're paying me to be your bodyguard, not to like you. I can't help you on that front. Not when you go around bragging and making up crazy shit like that."

His face crumples and drains of color.

"Markus, that was a little harsh," I say quickly. "I'm sorry—"

Markus suddenly stands and pushes his way through the crowd to the front door. He's gone into the darkness before I can catch him.

"What's up with your freaky little buddy?" says Alex, dislodging himself from the crowd to stand beside me. I shrug.

"Well, you should probably go get him." Alex pats me on the back. "You're on his payroll, right?"

"I don't care about the money. You can't pay me enough to deal with this."

Alex says, "Seriously, dude? You're going to just let him go? That's cold." I guess he's right. As I leave the house, I hear Alex shout after me, "You should really ask for a raise!"

Chapter Nine

It should be easy to spot him. Pools of light from the streetlamps dot the road in either direction. It's quiet except for the gentle rush of wind through the leaves of oak trees.

Then I hear the *slap-slap* of shoes hitting pavement. He's about a block away, running hard down the sidewalk.

I shake my head again. I'm really not getting paid enough for this. I switch into sprint mode. He's no match for me. I've almost caught up as he reaches the next intersection.

"Markus!" I shout.

I see him hesitate and then come to a stop in the middle of the road. He turns around to squint back at me. All of a sudden Markus is illuminated by a bright white light. There's a low mechanical hum. A big black Lexus comes roaring out of the darkness. Straight at Markus.

He swivels around to stare at the oncoming car. He raises his arms up, like he can shield himself from the two tons of vehicle that's about to crush him.

With a surge of adrenaline and speed, I cover the distance between us in seconds. I launch myself into the air and tackle Markus. We tumble to the other side of the road just as the black

Lexus rushes by, tires screeching on the pavement.

I roll away from Markus and sit up. My left arm aches where I hit the pavement hard. The Lexus is paused just past the intersection, idling. The windows are rolled down, and I can see the driver staring at me. But he's in the shadows. I'm under a bright streetlight. I can't make out what he looks like. No doubt he got a good look at me. He kicks the car into gear and takes off. Exhaust stings my nose.

Markus groans, still lying on the street. He has a cut on his forehead that's oozing bright red blood. "That was him," says Markus. "The Plunger."

We limp back to Alex's house, nervously listening for the sound of the Lexus. But it doesn't return to finish us off. This time when we knock, it's Alex who answers the door.

"Whoa. You guys get into a dustup?" he says when he sees us. Markus has a bloody hand pressed against the wound on his head. I'm cradling my injured arm.

"No, it wasn't me versus him," I say. "It was car versus us." I glare at Markus. "I think there are a few more stories we need to hear. Can we come in?"

Little red drops of blood speckle the white tile of the master bathroom.

"Can you wipe that up?" Alex says to me. He's busy sticking a fat bandage across Markus's forehead. "You know, if my DJ career doesn't work out, I might just become a doctor. I'm damn good at this."

Markus doesn't look so certain. He squirms on the bathroom floor as Alex works on him. Emily hands me some tissue, and I wipe up the blood. "So there really is someone out to get you?" I ask Markus.

Markus rolls his eyes, then winces. "It is what I have told you all the time. I tell you all the truth."

"Hang on," says Emily. "You said this Russian guy specializes in drowning people in the Hudson. That's like, New York City."

"Jersey, actually," mumbles Markus.

"Fine. Either way, it's nowhere near Estonia." She crosses her arms and looks at him with a raised eyebrow.

"Emily, he said he was from Narnia," says Alex. He turns to me. "I didn't think it was a real place either. Isn't that what you said?"

I nod.

It's Emily's turn to roll her eyes. "You're both idiots." She turns her attention back to Markus, who's looking sheepish. "So what's the real deal, Mr. Estonia? Or Mr. Jersey?"

"I told you the truth before," he says plaintively, "Only now I will tell you more truth."

"The more truth, the better."

Markus shifts around on the bathroom floor, trying to get comfortable. "My parents are from Estonia, but we moved to Jersey three years ago, after my father got a job there. It was very lonely. I am the only child in my family, and it was difficult for me to make friends."

"I can see that," I say. "No offense."

Markus shrugs. "So I spent much time doing two things. Playing games online, mainly poker on websites. And programming computers. Writing code. Then I discovered I could combine both things."

"I think I see where this is going," says Alex. He packs the medical kit back into a little red bag. "You're a... poker hacker?"

Markus pauses, then nods. "That is a good description. I learned how to write a program that let me—"

"Cheat?" says Emily.

"Not cheat. I did not break the law. My program let me predict what other players were probably going to do. I was able to win many games. And make much money."

That explained the nice clothes. The fact that he could afford a bodyguard.

"So how does the Plunger fit into all this?" Alex says.

"When I met him, I did not know him as the Plunger. He was just Yuri. I met him online. I was bragging about what I had done, and he was so impressed. I thought he wanted to be my friend. He lived in Jersey, and I did not know anybody else."

I feel a little sorry for Markus, so desperate for a friend that he fell into a mess like this.

Markus continues. "Yuri gave me money to play with. In return, I would make more money for him. Each time I could improve my code a little bit. I did not care about the money, but Yuri did. One day he brought me a gym bag full of cash. He told me to make a bank account and put the money into it. Use it for betting online. It was too much. When I told him this, he said I could not say no."

"He made you an offer you couldn't refuse?" says Alex. "Just like the movie! That's awesome."

"No. Less than awesome. This is when I found out that Yuri is part of a Russian gangster family." Markus shakes his head sadly. "Yuri told me my parents would have an accident with the Hudson River if I did not work with him."

"That would have been a good time to call the cops or the FBI or something," says Emily.

"Yes," says Markus, nodding. "But then I thought about what would happen. Maybe I was an accidental criminal, but still…I had used mobster money to gamble. My father was only in America on a temporary visa. He would lose his job. We would be sent back to Estonia."

"So you took Yuri's bag of money," I say.

"Yes, but I did not put it in the bank. I wrote Yuri an email saying I would give back the money if my parents were not hurt. I kept the money as insurance and ran away to where he would not find me. I found the smallest town in the middle of a very big nowhere."

This did not sound like a good plan at all. But I didn't say that out loud.

"You mean here? Marathon?" says Alex. "Watch what you say about my town."

"It's a harsh yet accurate description, sweetie," says Emily. "But Markus, aren't your parents looking for you?"

He squirms. "I never lie to them, but this was for their safety, no? I told them I was going on a cultural-exchange trip for a few weeks. I changed the school computers to make this happen." He smiles and flashes his braces at her. "I'm very good with computers."

"Well, you apparently didn't run far enough. Whoever was driving that Lexus wanted to make a point. It was no accident." I stand up and stretch, my arm throbbing a little less than before. "I'll drive you home."

Markus waits for me on the porch as kids drift away from the party. The music is off, and the cleanup crew is working to hide all the evidence. I'm about to leave

75

when Alex grabs my shoulder. He leans in and whispers.

"That story of his, it sounds totally like a movie. Like, I don't know if I believe it."

"I know." I lift up my arm with its new purple bruise. "But someone definitely wants to hurt him."

Chapter Ten

In my dream I am running from a big black car chasing me. The sound of my feet gets louder and louder. Like a drumbeat inside my head.

Then I wake up and realize someone is pounding on my bedroom door.

"Ryan!" shouts my mom's muffled voice. "You have ten minutes to get yourself dressed, brushed and otherwise cleaned up. Mr. Howards is going to be here in less than half an hour!"

I stare at the ceiling, heart still racing from the dream. Mr. Howards. The recruiter from Ryeburn College. Visiting me today. Mom and Dad must be losing their minds with excitement. Me, I've got that queasy feeling that I get before a big game. Riding the vomit comet, as Alex would say.

When I make it downstairs, Mom and Dad are buzzing around the living room. The place looks spotless. All the clutter that marks our everyday life has been removed and replaced with staged family photos and sparkling polished trophies. There are football magazines arranged neatly on the coffee table.

Amber wanders in and sprawls across the couch, tapping at her phone. Dad growls at her, but before it can erupt into a proper disaster, the doorbell chimes. Amber looks startled and swivels around to sit properly. Mom rushes to the door.

"Mr. Howards!" I hear her say. "So wonderful to finally meet you!"

She leads him into the living room. He's a short little guy, coming only up to my nose. He's wearing a brown suit and a bow tie. He smiles at me from under his bushy mustache.

"You must be Ryan," he says, offering his hand. "We are so excited to talk to you." It takes a couple of minutes to get coffee served, with Mom and Dad almost stumbling over each other to offer milk and sugar to Mr. Howards. Finally, Mom, Dad and Amber arrange themselves in a line on the couch. Mr. Howards and I each sit in an armchair, facing each other on opposite sides of the coffee table.

"Now I want to make clear that this is still not an official visit. We'll need to get you up to the Ryeburn campus to see our facilities. You need to meet the coaching staff, all of that sort of thing. Today is just the first step in a, well, a journey that we hope you will undertake with Ryeburn College."

"Go, Ryeburn Rattlers!" says Dad. Mr. Howards smiles like he's heard that a few times before. Dad tries to recover. "The fields and the gym at Ryeburn look first-rate," he says. "The pictures online are terrific. Did you use drones to take that footage?"

"Thank you. I don't know about any drones." Mr. Howards focuses on me. He pulls out a little notebook and pen. "Ryan, the point of this visit is to get to know you a little better, you know, off the field. So why don't you tell me a bit about yourself. What's a quality that you're most proud of?"

"Dedication to his team," says Mom. "He's always there for everyone else. Always thinking about other players. He really puts the team first."

"Ryan knows that there is no *I* in team," adds Dad.

"That's because he learned to *s-p-e-l-l* a long time ago," mutters Amber. Dad narrows his eyes at her.

"All right then, Ryan," says Mr. Howards. "Tell me, what do you love about the game?"

"Scoring a touchdown—" starts Dad.

"Ryan…" Mr. Howards holds up a hand and looks at me. "I need to hear from you, Ryan. What do you love about the game?"

My stomach is way past butterflies—now it's grinding up gravel. I barely got any sleep last night. Mom and Dad are acting crazy. All of this feels like one bad dream that keeps going on.

"Honestly, Mr. Howards?" I find myself saying. "I like football. I'm good at football. But I don't *love* the game."

You know that look in horror movies when someone finally sees the creature? That reaction shot as the poor victim is about to scream in full-on terror at the monster in front of them? That is pretty much the expression on Mom and Dad's faces.

Mr. Howards just tips his head to one side. "You don't? So why do you play football then?"

"Like I said, I'm good at it. And I love being on a team. I love being able to score a touchdown, because it makes so many people happy. But I don't actually like football. It makes me want to puke. Literally."

"Huh," says Mr. Howards. "Well, Ryan, I appreciate your honesty. Never heard that one before." He scribbles in his little notebook.

"Well, what Ryan means to say—" says Mom.

"No, Mom. I said what I mean."

She winces. For a moment I think she might cry. But it's too late. I can't stop.

"To be honest, sir, I don't know if I want to play football for the rest of my life. Or even in college. There's a lot of options out there. I'm only eighteen."

Dad looks lost. He opens and closes his mouth without making any sound.

Mr. Howards fills the silence. "What kind of other things are you interested in? Maybe there's a program at Ryeburn that you'd like, something in addition to football." He looks at me, pen poised over his notebook.

"Film. Making movies. I think that's what I want to do more than anything. More than football."

"Ah. Unfortunately, we don't have a film program," says Mr. Howards.

He's smiling at me, but it's a sad smile. "There are a lot of young men your age who do love the game and really, truly want to win a scholarship to Ryeburn. I've seen you play on the field. You have great potential. Unofficially, I'd even say that you're good enough to receive a full ride. But we're not going to give it to you unless you really want it."

Mr. Howards flips the notebook closed and stands up. "It was very nice to meet you, Ryan. I hope you will think hard about what you want to do and then get back to me." He sticks out a hand for me to shake, smiling under his bushy mustache.

Needless to say, Mom and Dad lose their minds after Mr. Howards leaves. It's like the nuclear version of family arguments, no survivors left standing. I fire off some heavy-duty ammunition.

I only ever played football to make them happy and I hated every minute of it. Boom.

Dad just wants to use me to relive his glory days of college football. Because basically he's a has-been. Boom.

If either one of them actually cared about me, they'd have listened to me sometime over the past decade. Boom.

In return, they drop a couple of their own bombshells. I'm a selfish, lazy son who can't be bothered to use the gifts he's been given. How could I throw away my chance at a scholarship when our family doesn't have the money to send me to college? Why would I destroy my life to make stupid little movies that will never amount to anything?

That last one sends me out of the living room like I've been fired from a cannon. I grab my backpack with the camera in it, slam out the front door and take off down the street. The anger inside me is like a humming engine, driving me along faster and faster. Soon I find myself running, block after block, not caring where I end up.

Chapter Eleven

I'm staring through the glass storefront at a display television, an expensive wide-screen digital one. It's showing a repeat of *Saturday Night Football*, a game between Texas A&M and Florida State. I don't want to go home, but my legs ache from running. At least there's a game to watch.

Suddenly I notice the ghost of a black car in the window. The reflection of a black Lexus behind me, across the street. I can't see the driver, but I'm sure he's staring at me. I casually turn away from the storefront and start walking down the sidewalk. I hear the rumble of the engine as the car starts up. Reaching an intersection, I fake a right turn, then spin left and run down the side street. The soreness in my legs is forgotten as I tear along. There's a screech as the Lexus accelerates to catch up. I pour it on even more, sprinting down the sidewalk, dodging a woman with a stroller, a dog walker, a homeless guy. The Lexus keeps pace with me. Then I see my opportunity—a back alley that's too narrow for a car. I slip into it, and the Lexus disappears from sight. Breathing heavily, I sneak a look back on the street. It's gone.

Then I see a black Lexus creeping down the street. Just as I start to panic, I realize that it's being driven by an old lady with gray hair. Her golden retriever is riding shotgun beside her. Probably not a Russian mobster. I ease out of the alley, head swiveling back and forth. Another black Lexus. No, just something similar. A bunch of little kids in the back, dad up front. I rub my eyes. *Get a grip*. I'm jumping at shadows. Maybe I wasn't being followed at all. I've been acting insane all day. Screwing up my future. The crazy is rubbing off on me. I really need to talk to Markus.

As part of the "cultural exchange" he arranged, Markus is staying with a host family across town. I climb up the creaky steps to their covered porch and bang on the screen door. Markus appears.

"Replay? I thought you could not protect me today, because you had the meeting with the football person, right?" He looks at me through the screen door, puzzled.

"Yeah, that." I slowly shrug. "It didn't go so well. I think I just blew up my future."

"You will need to explain more." Markus still looks confused. "But I have been inside hiding all day. If you are here, I would like to be outside. The park is across the street." He dips out of sight, then pops back up with an old football. "You can protect me and show me how to throw the skinny pig." He steps outside to join me.

"Pigskin." I smile. I drop my backpack to the wooden floor of the porch and hold my hands out. "Pass."

While I'm trying to teach Markus a spiral, I tell him about the recruiter.

My parents. How my future plans have unraveled.

"It sounds like"—Markus heaves the ball, which tumbles end over end—"you have decided that you do not want to play football. You must make your movies instead."

"You think?" I say sarcastically, retrieving the ball. "Except that's not going to happen. I spent the whole day thinking about it. I can't let my parents down like that. I don't even have the hundred and fifty bucks to apply to film school. It's a stupid idea." I underhand-pass to Markus. "I've got to apologize to Mr. Howards, make it right."

Dressed in black jeans and a loose T-shirt, Markus looks like a scarecrow out on the green big green field. He actually catches it this time and smiles broadly. Then he wraps his hand around the ball again, spreading his finger along the seam like I taught him. He reaches back to throw, then pauses. "But that is not what you really want. I think you must be like…who is the boss of the football team?"

"The quarterback?" I say.

Markus throws. The ball dribbles away into the grass. He sighs and turns to face me.

"The quarterback. I know these words, but together they make no sense. Anyway, yes. This is the one who decides on the plan for the team, yes?" He raises his eyebrows. "You must decide on your plan. Your parents are not the quarterbackers. You are."

"Markus, I'm not sure I should be coming to you for advice. You hang out with gangsters, steal their money and lie to your parents."

"This is true," Markus says. "It was sort of an accident?"

"That Lexus was no accident," I say, scooping up the ball. "I don't think you planned to do the wrong thing. You just kind of wandered into it."

Markus takes his glasses off and polishes them on his shirt. "This is also true. But now my plan is a good one. To run away from the Plunger."

"Except that he's already found you." I pick up the ball and toss it from hand to hand. "You going to keep running forever? Never go home again?"

A flash of anger passes over Markus's face, then fades. "Maybe I need a better plan," he says.

I throw the ball, which Markus fumbles. "Is it all right if I take tomorrow morning off from being a bodyguard? I think I need to sort things out at home."

Markus nods. He doesn't look like a scarecrow anymore. Just a lost little kid, standing in the empty field.

When I eventually get home, there is a plate of food waiting for me on the kitchen table. No angry voices. No annoyed note. Just room-temperature macaroni and a silent house. Somehow that's worse.

Chapter Twelve

Dad hands me a list of chores without saying a word. Mom still isn't speaking to me either. Amber is, for once, keeping quiet and lying low. I think everybody is afraid that any conversation might end up with a full-on disaster like we had yesterday. So we all just keep our mouths shut.

Halfway through the day I realize that the backpack with my camera in it is missing. I must have left it on the porch at Markus's place.

I text him. No response. An hour later I text him again. Then I try and call him. Again no response. Weird. It's like he's giving me the silent treatment as well.

When I finally finish my chores, it's already early afternoon. I ask to borrow the car and Dad narrows his eyes but hands me the keys. I drive back to Markus's and knock on the screen door. His host mother answers and tells me that Markus isn't home.

"He left around lunchtime with his brother. Seemed such a nice surprise for him, to see his brother again."

"His brother?"

"Yes, a nice young man with an accent too. He seemed so happy to catch up with Markus. They were going to spend the day together, maybe have dinner." She sees my face and looks concerned. "Is everything all right?"

"Sure, just sorry to have missed him. Thanks." I turn away but then remember why I came over. "Oh, I think I left my backpack here on the porch yesterday." We both look around, but it's nowhere to be found. While the woman goes to look for it inside, I start pacing around the porch, my thoughts racing. I try to put together the pieces. Why did Markus never mention having a brother? I feel the muscles in my neck start to tense, like when I see a play going wrong on the field.

The woman returns with my back-pack. "Success! Markus is a lovely boy, but his bedroom is a mess. I found it under a pile of clothes." She shakes her head and hands the backpack to me. I realize it's heavier than before—I only had my little video camera in it, but now it feels like it has a couple bricks inside.

Back in the car, I tug open the backpack. There's my camera, resting on top of…what? Not bricks but something the same size and shape. I reach inside and feel dense bundles of paper. Cash. I pull a wad out, amazed. This backpack has more bills than I've ever seen before in one place.

I text Markus right away.

WTF? Where are you? What's with the cash?

No answer. I squint at the little glowing screen like I can somehow force Markus to call me. Nothing. I turn the keys in the ignition and chuck the phone to the passenger seat in disgust. I crank on the radio, turning it too loud in frustration, and rev the motor.

Which means I almost miss the buzz of the phone as it rings. I kill the engine and scramble for the phone.

"Markus! What the hell is going on?"

The voice at the other end of the line is deep and resonant. And not Markus's.

"No need to worry. He is safe with me."

"Who is this?" I see my reflection in the rearview mirror, pale and wide-eyed.

"I am business partner of Markus." The accent is similar to Markus's. He speaks the same way, very precisely and carefully. "To be accurate, I am a former business partner. In fact, I have only one financial transaction left with our mutual friend."

"What are you talking about?"

"I should use smaller words for you, no?" He laughs. "You are a football player, after all. Markus told me that you were his bodyguard."

It all comes together. "You're Yuri. The Plunger."

I hear him hiss on the other end of the line. "Do not call me that. In English that is stupid name. In Russian it sounds much better." Hearing his frustration gives me a boost of bravery. Or stupidity.

"Listen, Plunger, I don't know what's going on, but maybe I just better call the cops right now."

"You may be a football player, but you are not that dumb, are you? Your friend is a criminal. And from the text you just sent, I believe you are in possession of stolen money. You think the police will assume you are innocent in all of this, *Ryan*?"

"How do you know who I am?"

"Markus and I have had many conversations over the past few hours. He even gave me a tour of Marathon. Your school. Your house. The one thing he did not reveal to me is where my money was. But now I know you have it. So let us do business, without any police. I would like to arrange a trade."

"You want the money."

"Yes. In return I will give Markus back to you. As his bodyguard"—he snickers—"it does seem like the least you can do for him."

"Fine. But I want to speak to him. Make sure he's all right."

There's just empty static for a moment while Yuri considers this. "It is acceptable. Here." I hear the muffled sound of the phone being passed from hand to hand.

"Replay?" Markus's voice sounds thin and distant.

"Has he hurt you? Are you all right?"

"I am okay but so sorry for you. I did not mean for this to happen."

"Whatever. Look, I just want to get this money back to Yuri."

"No! If you do that," Markus says quickly, "I will not be able to protect my family. There will be nothing stopping Yuri from threatening them, forcing me to work for him. Do not give him—"

There's a grunt. Then Yuri is back on the line. "I hope you are more clever than Markus. Bring the money to your school football field. Nine o'clock tonight. Come alone." The line disconnects with a beep.

Chapter Thirteen

My room is bathed in a blue-white light. The shades are drawn, and I'm hunched over my laptop. Clip after clip of footage scrolls by on the screen. Screaming crowds from the game. A solid mass of people surging in time to the beat at the pool party. Alex's big goofy grin as he photobombs a shot of the game. I've been watching this stuff all afternoon. Like I can use all the little fragments I've recorded over the past week to somehow find an answer to the big question. What am I going to do?

Call the cops. Hand the entire problem over to someone else to figure out. Hope that they don't figure I'm one of the bad guys. Probably ruin any shot of a scholarship once the word gets out that I'm involved with people like Yuri.

Be a hero. Take down the Plunger and rescue Markus. Get shot, drowned or some horrible combination of the two. Like an action-movie hero, only super sad and depressing.

Hide in my room and try to avoid making any decisions at all. Run down the clock and wait for someone else to make the decision for me.

I jump at a knock at my door, startled out of my trance.

"Ryan?" It's Dad. I feel my chest tighten up. I don't want a fight right now.

But he knocks again. And again. I finally give up, rolling my desk chair over to open up the door.

Dad peers past me into the shadowy room. "Well, this doesn't look suspicious at all. You sitting in the dark in the middle of a Sunday afternoon," he says. Seeing the glow of the screen, he adds, "You looking at something you shouldn't?" He's half-joking.

"No, nothing like that." I roll aside to let him in. "I was just editing some footage."

Dad walks over to the laptop. On the screen is a clip of him and Mom at the game. They are both frozen mid-cheer, their gold wigs completing their shimmery Warrior outfits. He snorts.

"Yikes. Can't you fix up those old people with one of your fancy programs? Make them look a little younger?" Dad squints at the screen. "Maybe a lot younger?"

I laugh, feeling the tightness in my chest loosen up. "I'm afraid there's no app for that."

Dad laughs too. He turns back to me, smiling. "Ryan, I've been thinking about what you said yesterday. About how I've been making you play football because...because that's what I always wanted. Not what *you* wanted."

"Dad, I didn't—"

"Let me finish. I think you might have been partly right." He sits on my bed. The springs squeak. "When I watch you play, I feel...joy in my heart. There's no other word for it. And part of that comes from me remembering that feeling. Rushing down the field like an angel taking flight." He punches a finger in the air. "Unstoppable."

I smile a little, seeing him all worked up like this. He chuckles, then continues.

"I had that feeling, once or twice. You have it every game, I bet. But the joy that I feel watching you? It's because *you're* doing something that you have a gift for. I'd feel the same way if your gift was…was playing the trombone."

I raise an eyebrow.

"Not sure where that came from. I'm not a fan of the trombone. But I would feel joy if playing it was your gift," he insists. "I do admit, the fact that you are so good at a game that I love so much, well, that blinded me a little. Your mom too. I didn't pay as much attention to the other stuff you were good at. Like this." He jerks a thumb at the laptop.

"It's okay, Dad. I went along with it. I mean, being a football star has some upside," I say.

"Yeah, I bet it does. But now that you're graduating, I want to make one thing clear." Dad stands up and puts a hand on my shoulder. "From here on in, it's your call. You decide what you're going to do with your gifts. Your mother and I are on your team, one hundred percent."

"Thanks," I say.

Neither of us knows what to do next. Dad turns to leave. Maybe I should let him in on what's going on with Markus.

"Hey, Dad. There's something else." He turns slowly back. I think about what Yuri said, about how he knows where I live. Mom and Dad might be on my team, but that doesn't mean they need to take the risk with me. I change my mind.

"There's this trombone I want to buy," I say. "Maybe you can help me out?"

He laughs and closes the door behind him. I swivel back to the screen.

It's my call. Like Markus said, I'm the quarterback. Time to start calling the play.

Chapter Fourteen

I'm in the tunnel that leads to the field, the white stadium lights from the field spilling into the shadows.

"You're sure you know what to do?" I whisper to Alex, probably for the tenth time.

"Replay, I've got this." Alex rolls his eyes.

"If you want to back out, I can handle this on my own. I mean, maybe it's not a good plan. You should just—"

"Dude." Alex grabs me. "Do you need to ride the vomit comet? Have a little pre-game puke session to get the nerves out?"

My face loosens into a smile. "No, I'm fine."

"It's a good plan. Stick with it." Alex slaps me on the back. "Now get out there."

I take a deep breath, lift the backpack onto my shoulders and start walking into the brilliant light of the empty stadium.

When Yuri shows up I'm waiting at the fifty-yard line. He appears at the north entrance to the field, shoving Markus ahead of him. Yuri is a big guy, broad shoulders wrapped in a black motorcycle jacket with a low collar, head shaved to look tough. He pretty much looks just like I imagined—except for his age. He can't be more than a year or two older than I am.

Markus looks pale. He blinks a few times through his glasses, finally focusing on me. He shakes his head.

"Get away, Replay. Do not give him anything."

Yuri shoves Markus to his knees, and I step forward.

"Do not get closer," Yuri says. He gestures with one hand toward his open jacket. I can see the bulge of a handgun tucked into a holster. "You have my money?"

I nod, then shrug the backpack off and drop it at my feet. "Markus, come here."

Yuri grins. "No, no. I think that you do not give the orders. I get the money first, Mr. Football."

"That's not my name," I say. "It's Replay."

Yuri looks puzzled. "Replay? That is not a very tough-guy name."

"Well, the Plunger is a pretty crappy name. Literally," I say. From down on the grass, Markus snickers. Anger flashes across Yuri's face.

"Is much better in Russian. I did not know about the tool for the bathroom cleaning." He's almost whining, like a little kid. "See, the name means that I—"

"I know what it means," I say innocently. "It means that you believe in having a clean crapper that flushes well."

Markus looks up at me. "Replay, what are you doing?" he hisses.

"I'm calling an audible," I say quickly. "Remember what that means?" Markus looks confused. Yuri steps past Markus to get closer to me.

"You are insulting me? I do not think you understand what I am capable of. Do you know who my family is? Who I am?" There's a muscle under his left eye that's twitching.

"I know that you took your daddy's money and gave it to Markus here to play poker with. Now you want to keep him like some kind of trained pet. To keep making money for you." I step over the backpack so that we're inches away from each other. "I know you. You're a little kid pretending to be a tough guy. And I've protected Markus from worse."

Yuri growls and reaches into his jacket. Moments start flashing by in slow motion. Markus scrambles away from us, yelling. Yuri pulls out the gun. My pulse is racing, but I force myself not to move. I just stand there, hands at my side. Yuri carefully raises the barrel of the gun to my forehead.

"Do not insult me, Mr. Football." Yuri's hand is shaking a little, and he blinks furiously at me.

He might pretend to be a killer, but I don't think he's done this too many times before. Which doesn't actually make me feel any better, considering there's a gun pointed at my head. I swallow and try to speak as calmly as I can.

"That's not my name. It's Replay," I say. "Want to see why?"

I look up at the huge screen that hangs over the stadium. It suddenly flashes to life with a burst of static. Then an image snaps into focus. It's a live feed of Yuri pointing the gun at me. I made sure when I set up Alex with the camera that it would get a good view of Yuri's face.

"I have all of this on tape. You, threatening a defenseless kid with a gun that I'm betting isn't legal. That's got to be worth, what, a year in jail? Daddy would not be impressed."

Yuri quickly stuffs the gun back under his jacket, looking around.

"So here's the deal, Plunger." I toss the backpack at him. "You take your money and never contact Markus or me again. As long as you leave us alone, the tape will never be seen by anybody. You screw with me or Markus, or our families, or our friends? The tape goes straight to the Jersey police."

I'd expected Yuri to look furious, but instead he just looks really confused. He snatches at the backpack and sticks a hand inside to feel around for the money. Satisfied, he recovers some of his tough-guy act.

"We have a standoff for now, Mr. Replay." He points a finger at me. "Watch yourself."

After a quick look around at the empty stands, Yuri hustles for the exit.

A minute later we hear a car engine start, then fade into the distance. I kneel down and help Markus to his feet.

"You were most scary," says Markus.

"I was most terrified. But thank god it worked," I say.

Alex comes running out of the dark. "Dude, that was awesome! It was like the *Godfather*, but you're all, like—"

I know he's about to start acting it all out, and I shut him down.

"You can never say a word, you got it? This never happened."

Alex smiles. "Yeah, sure, man. Just keep some notes for your first blockbuster movie."

Chapter Fifteen

I open the door to see Markus standing there. He looks nervous. His formerly fancy gray jacket is now beaten up and smudged with dirt. Behind him I can see a car, the engine running. A man and woman watch us through the passenger window.

"Hello, Replay," says Markus. "I am on my way to the airport, but I made them stop. I must talk to you."

I gesture at the car. "Who are they? You okay?"

"They are my parents. They took a flight out here as soon as I called them."

"You told them what happened?" I ask.

"I told them a little piece of truth. That the exchange did not work out so well. That I am sick for home. Now we must return to Jersey." He shakes his head. "I am regretting my poker games. Perhaps I should have learned to play football?"

"I don't think that would have worked out for you either. No offense."

"It is true." He holds up a little envelope. "Also, I must give you this before I leave."

"Thanks." I take it. With everything that has happened, I had forgotten all about our deal.

Markus suddenly gives me an awkward hug. "Thank you," he says into my shoulder. "You are the best bodyguard."

"I don't know. You did get kidnapped, after all."

Markus nods. "Well, at least you are the best friend."

There's a honk from the car, and Markus lets go. "I must leave now. Be seeing you!"

When I'm back in my room, I look at the white envelope. It has *Reply* written across the front. I rip it open to find a bunch of bills and a little sticky note.

This is my money, not Yuri's. And this is not payment for Replay the Bodyguard. This is an investment in Ryan the Film Director. I can't wait to see your first film when it arrives in Jersey. Or even Estonia.
Your Friend, Markus

I laugh. It's a hundred and fifty bucks. Just enough to cover my film-school application. Mom and Dad are happy to help with the fee now, of course. But the money will definitely come in handy. I search around under the bed and find the crumpled-up application. I smooth it out on the desk.

Time to call my own play and see what happens.

Sean Rodman's interest in writing for teenagers came out of working at schools around the world. In Australia, he taught ancient history to future Olympic athletes. Closer to home, he worked with students from over 100 countries at a nonprofit international school. He is currently the executive director of the Story Studio Writing Society, a charity dedicated to unleashing the creativity of young writers and improving literacy. Sean lives in Victoria, British Columbia. For more information, visit srodman.com.